DC
SUPER
HEROES

BATMAN™

TALES OF THE BATCAVE

BATCAVE

THE JAGUAR'S JEWEL

by
MICHAEL DAHL

illustrated by
LUCIANO VECCHIO

Batman created by
BOB KANE WITH BILL FINGER

STONE ARCH BOOKS
a capstone imprint

Published by Stone Arch Books in 2018
A Capstone Imprint
1710 Roe Crest Drive
North Mankato, Minnesota 56003
www.mycapstone.com

STAR39738

Library of Congress Cataloging-in-Publication Data is available on the Library of
Congress website.

ISBN: 978-1-4965-5984-5 (hardcover)
ISBN: 978-1-4965-5996-8 (paperback)
ISBN: 978-1-4965-6009-4 (eBook PDF)

Summary: A series of false alarms at Gotham City's Museum of Geology leads Batman
and Robin to Catwoman and her plan to steal a cat-eyed jewel.

Editor: Christopher Harbo
Designer: Brann Garvey

Printed and bound in the USA.
010831S18

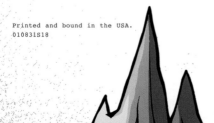

TABLE OF CONTENTS

This is the BATCAVE.

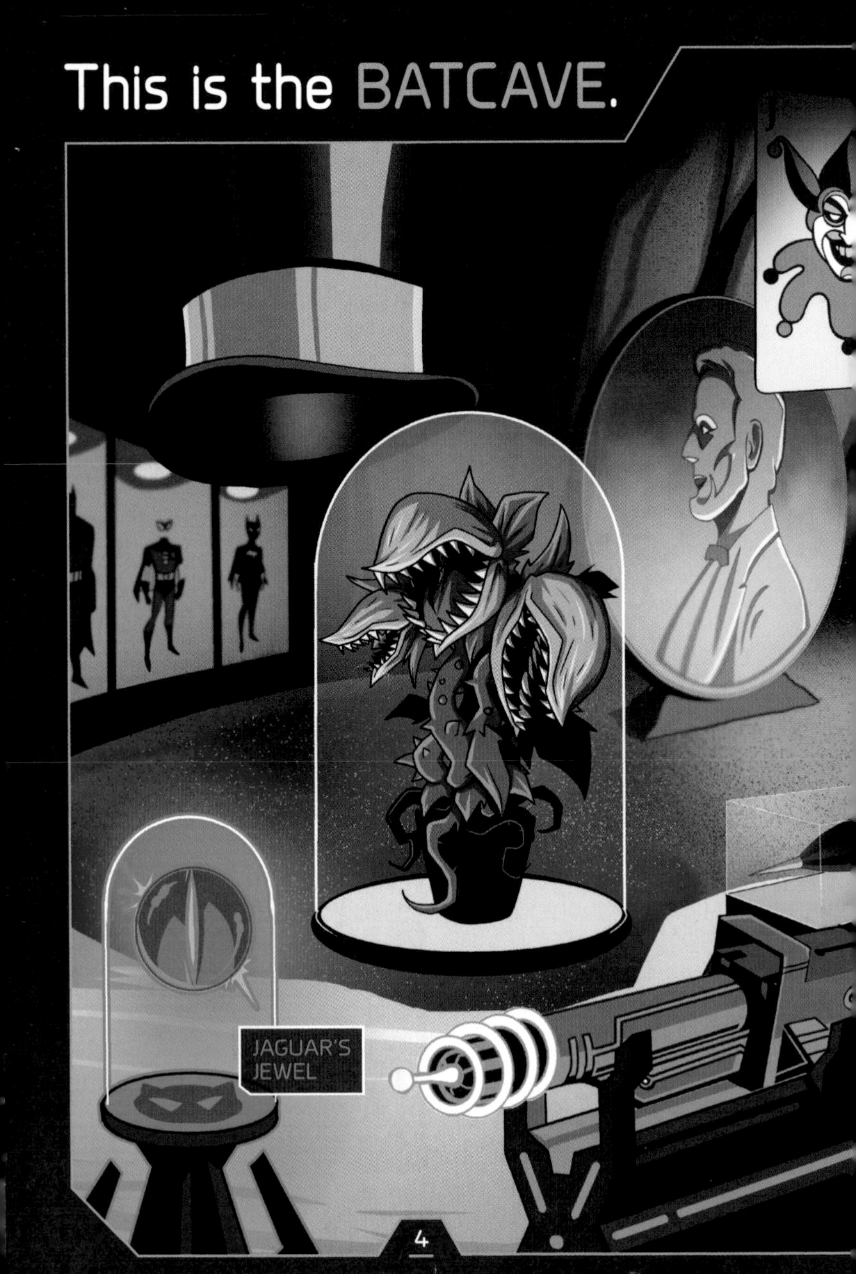
JAGUAR'S
JEWEL

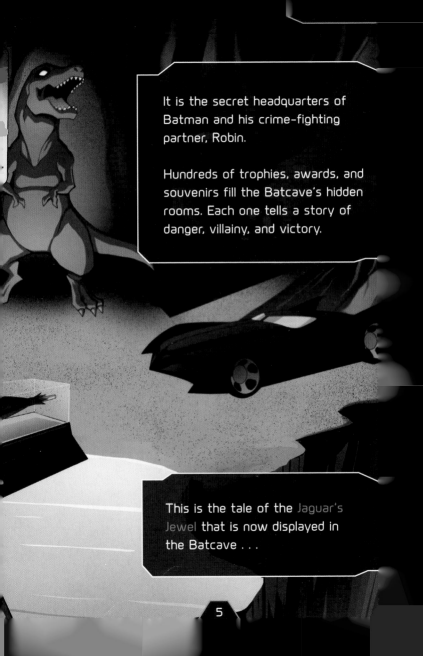

It is the secret headquarters of Batman and his crime-fighting partner, Robin.

Hundreds of trophies, awards, and souvenirs fill the Batcave's hidden rooms. Each one tells a story of danger, villainy, and victory.

This is the tale of the Jaguar's Jewel that is now displayed in the Batcave . . .

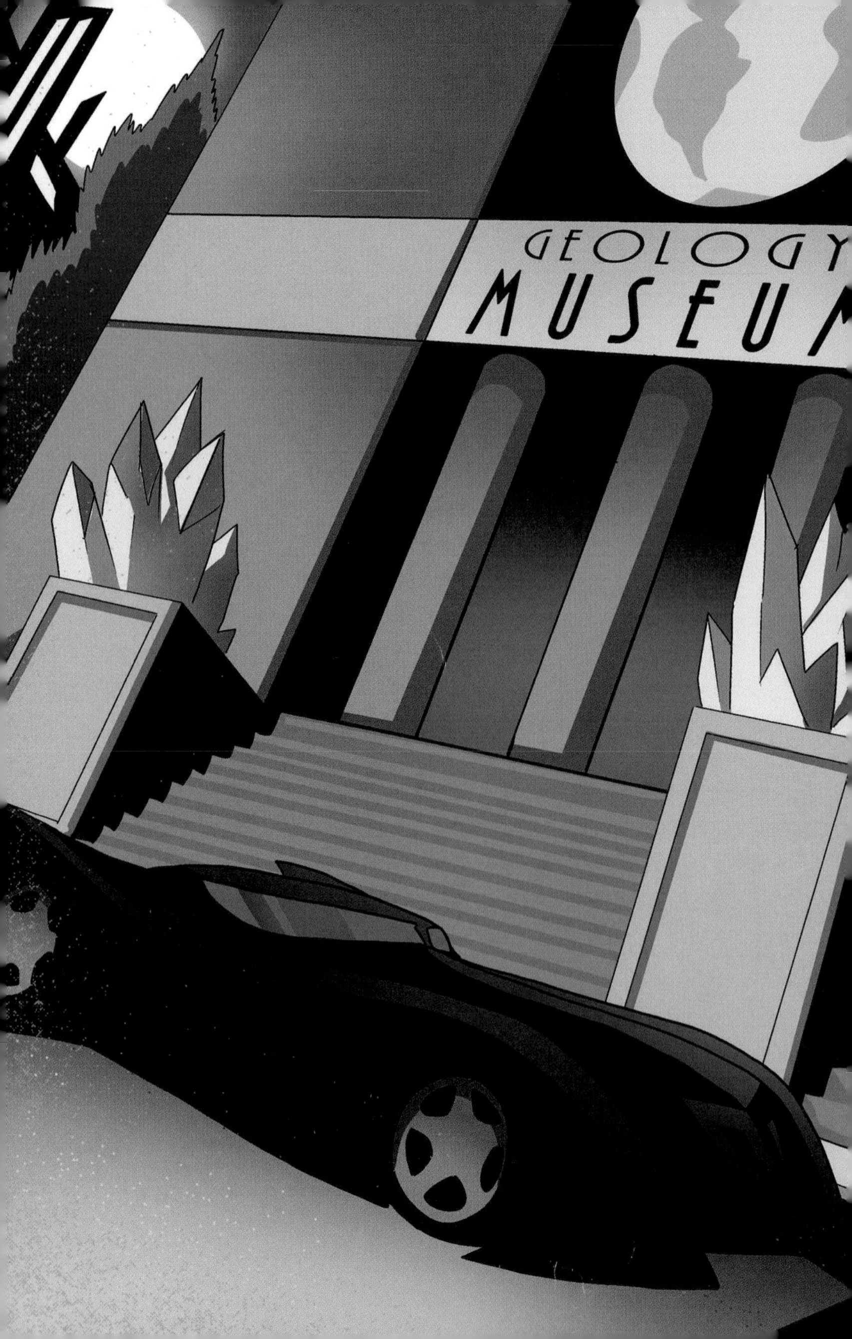
GEOLOGY
MUSEUM

CHAPTER 1

FALSE ALARM

REE-REE-REE-REEEE!

Gotham City is not having a quiet night.

An alarm blares at the Museum of Geology.

The Batmobile sits outside the museum.
The vehicle's powerful engine purrs.

Inside the building the Dynamic Duo run toward the source of the alarm.

"The Jaguar's Jewel has been stolen!" shouts the museum director.

The two crime fighters and the man race down a long hallway. They stop at a round glass case.

"The jewel," the man says again. "Thank goodness! It's still here!"

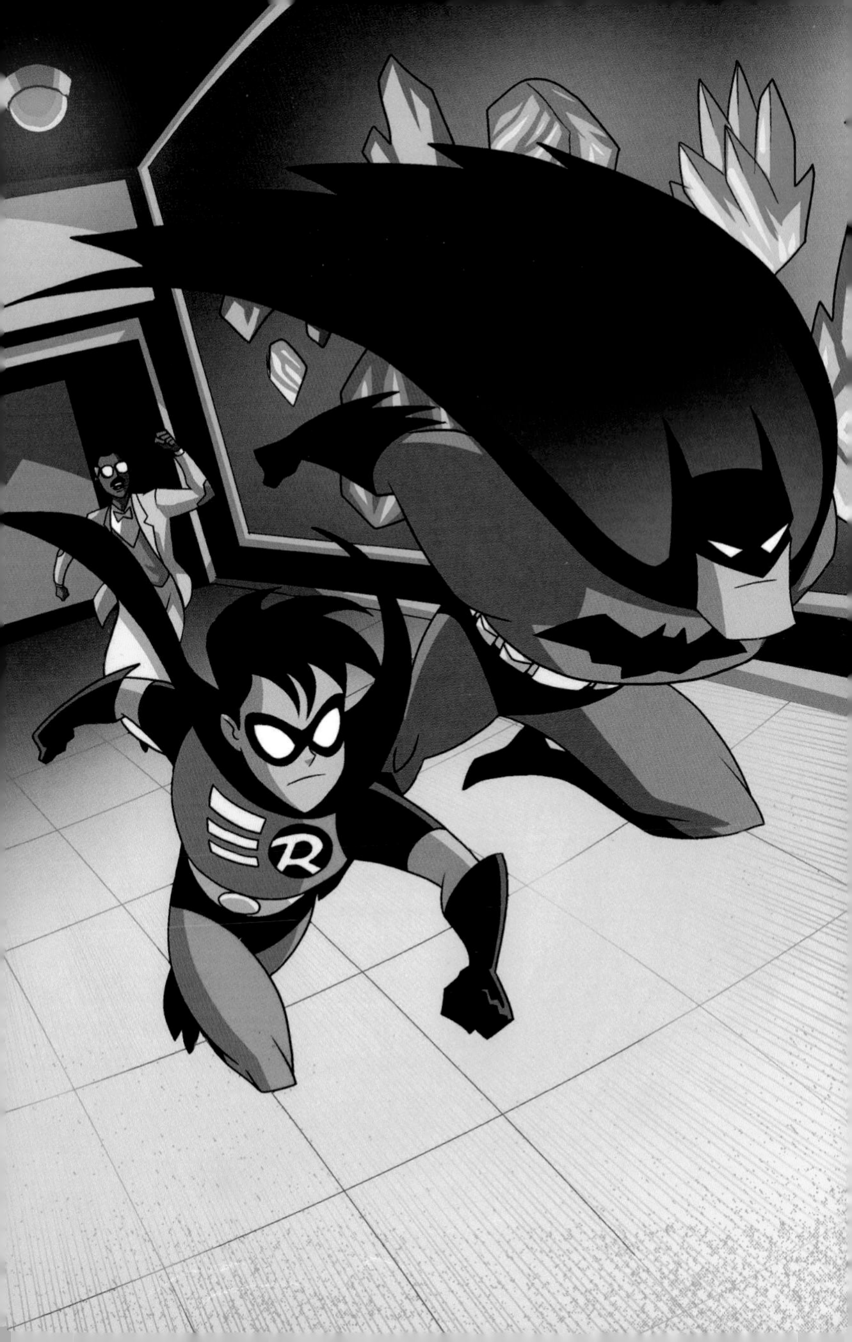

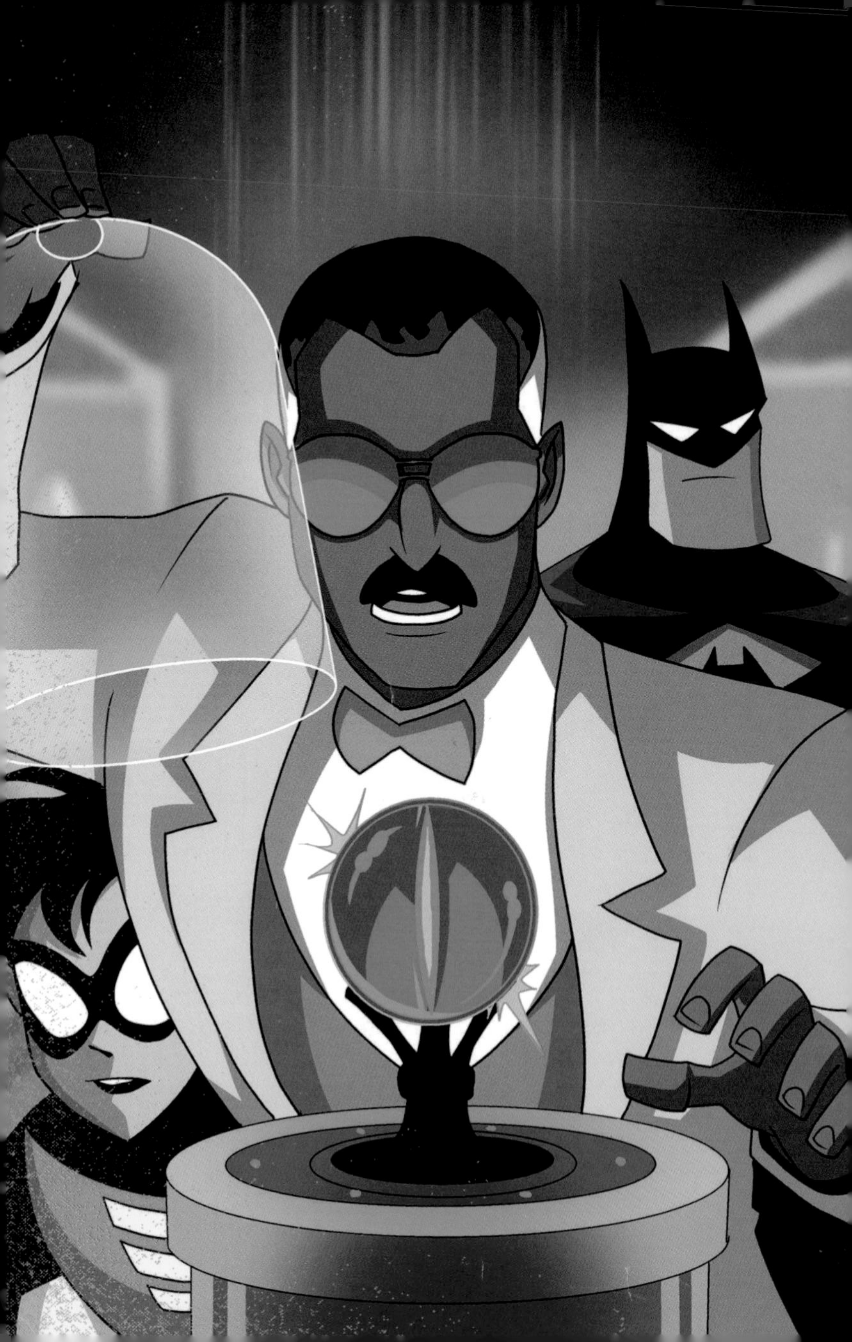

The emerald gleams inside the case. It is the size of an adult's fist and shaped like a huge cat's eye.

The director opens the case. He pulls out the gem and studies it closely.

"This is the real jewel, all right," he says.

"I don't understand," says Robin. "Why did the alarm go off?"

Two security guards, Juan and Sal, rush into the room.

"Nothing outside," Juan reports.

"All clear inside too," Sal says.

The alarm suddenly stops.

The director shakes his head. He replaces the green gem inside its case.

"Sorry, Batman," he says. "Sorry, Robin. This was a false alarm."

"I'm not so sure," says Robin. "This gem is the perfect catnip for that thief Catwoman."

Batman turns to the director. “We’ll stand guard here the rest of the night in case anything should happen,” he says.

But nothing does.

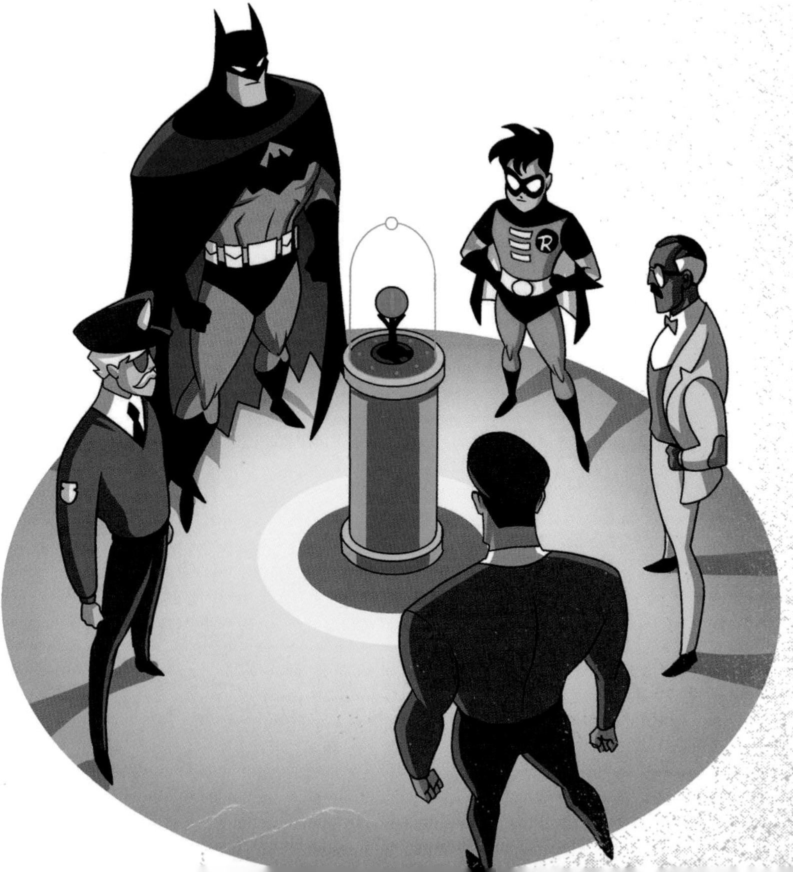

CHAPTER 2

NIGHT NUMBER NINE

Night after night the museum's alarm rings for no reason.

On the ninth night the alarm goes off again.

The security guards are tired of the noise. They turn off the alarm.

"That noise drives me nuts!" Juan says.

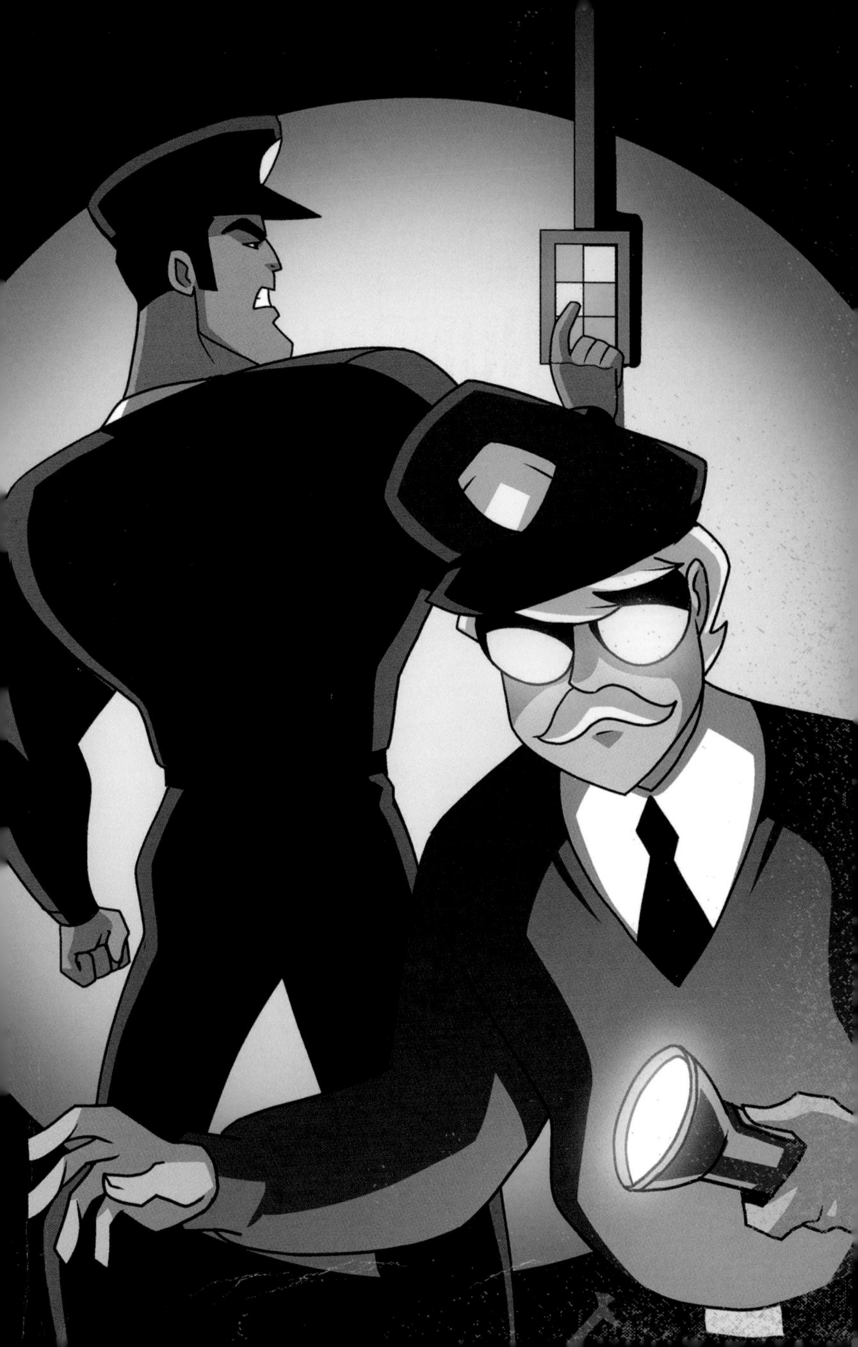

"I'll still go check things out," says Sal.

The young guard walks down a long, dark hallway. He reaches the room with the Jaguar's Jewel. The green gem is still safe.

The guard reaches in and pulls out the jewel. "Ahh, it's beautiful," he says.

Then the guard slips out of his uniform and his blond wig.

Sal is really Selina Kyle in disguise!

"I fooled them all," Selina says. Then she pulls the hood of her Catwoman uniform over her head.

"I even fooled the Dynamic Duo!"

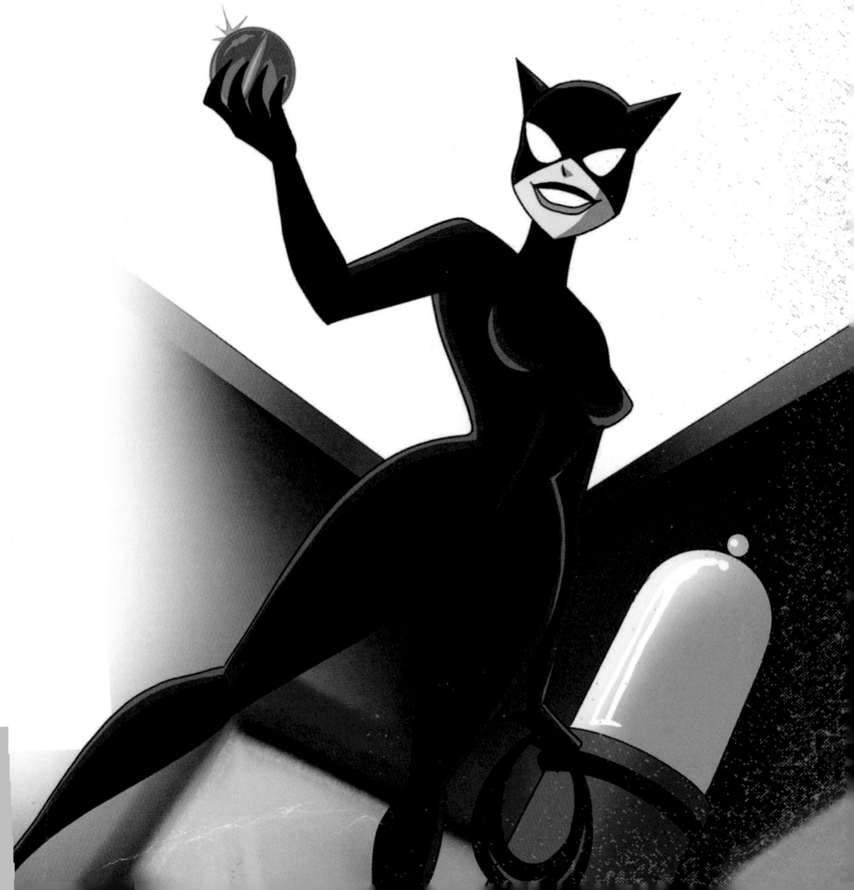

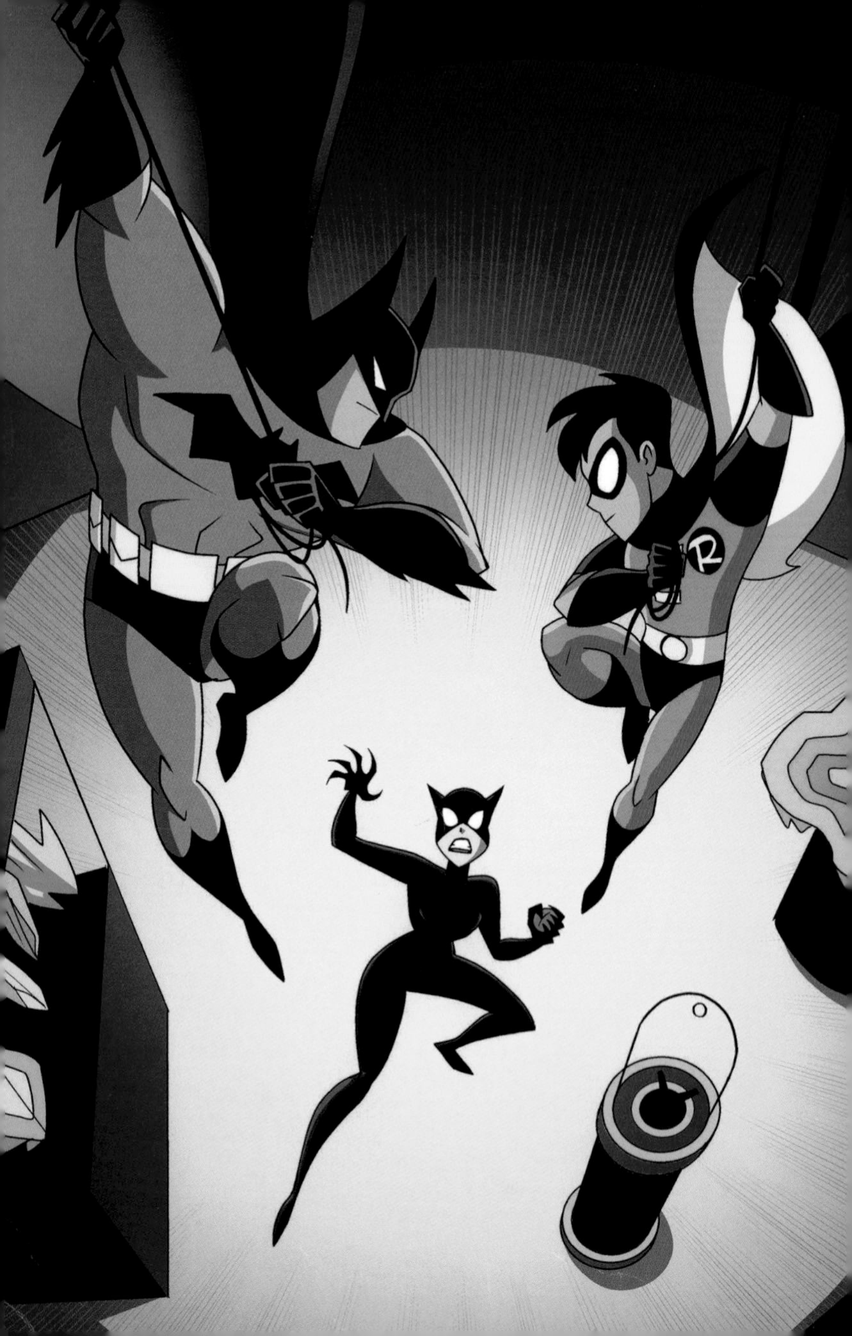

CHAPTER 3

THE JAGUAR WITH TWO EYES

SWISH!

A sudden noise causes Catwoman to look up. The Dynamic Duo swing down from the shadows on long ropes.

"Batman!" cries Catwoman.

The crime fighters land on the floor facing the thief.

"You thought we'd ignore the alarm if it went off every day," Batman says.

"But you were wrong," says Robin. "It went off for nine nights. Just like the nine lives of a cat."

"So you knew I was behind this," Catwoman says. "But do you know what is behind you?"

ROOO-OOO-OOARR!

The crime fighters turn around and see a real-life jaguar slinking out of the shadows.

The big cat flashes its green eyes. Its front paws spread their deadly claws.

"Wow! Where did that come from?" asks Robin.

"Bolivia," says Catwoman. "Her green eyes are quite rare. And she's very protective of me. Meow!"

Batman and Robin stand very still, facing the angry cat. They hear the echo of Catwoman's heels as she escapes down a dark hallway.

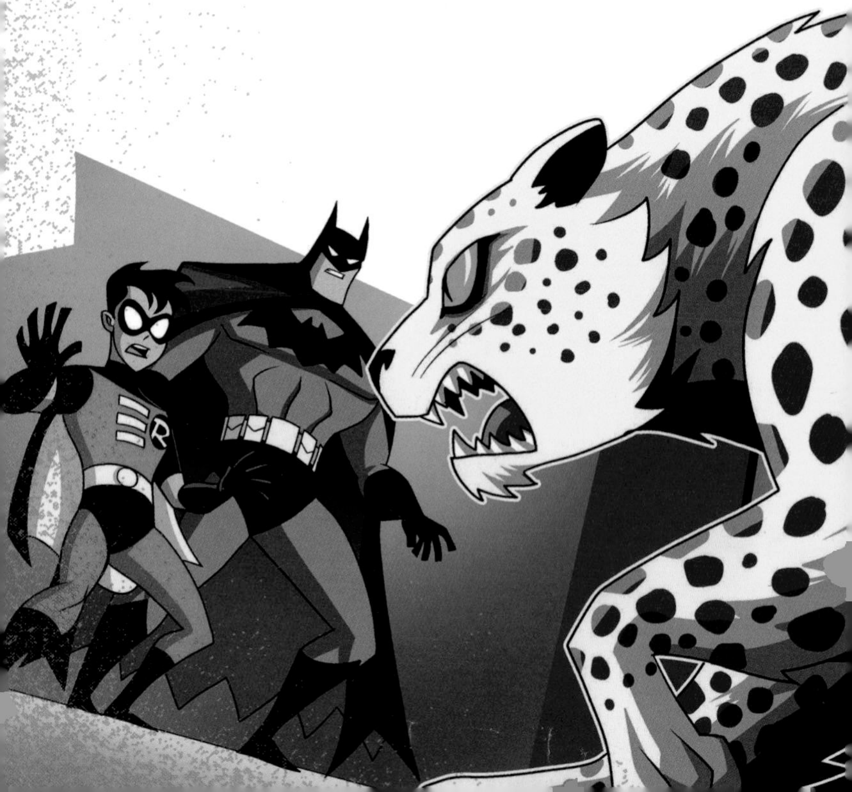

CHAPTER 4

ROBIN'S BRIGHT IDEA

SNAAARRRLLL!

The cat bares its teeth and moves closer.

Batman sees their ropes dangling from the ceiling. He knows the angry jaguar would be too fast. They would never reach the ropes in time.

"I'm all out of bright ideas," says Robin.

"That's it!" says Batman. "A bright light."

Carefully, without moving his body, Batman presses a button hidden in his glove. A small mirror pops into his hand.

The mirror reflects light from one of the room's lamps.

Robin does the same thing.

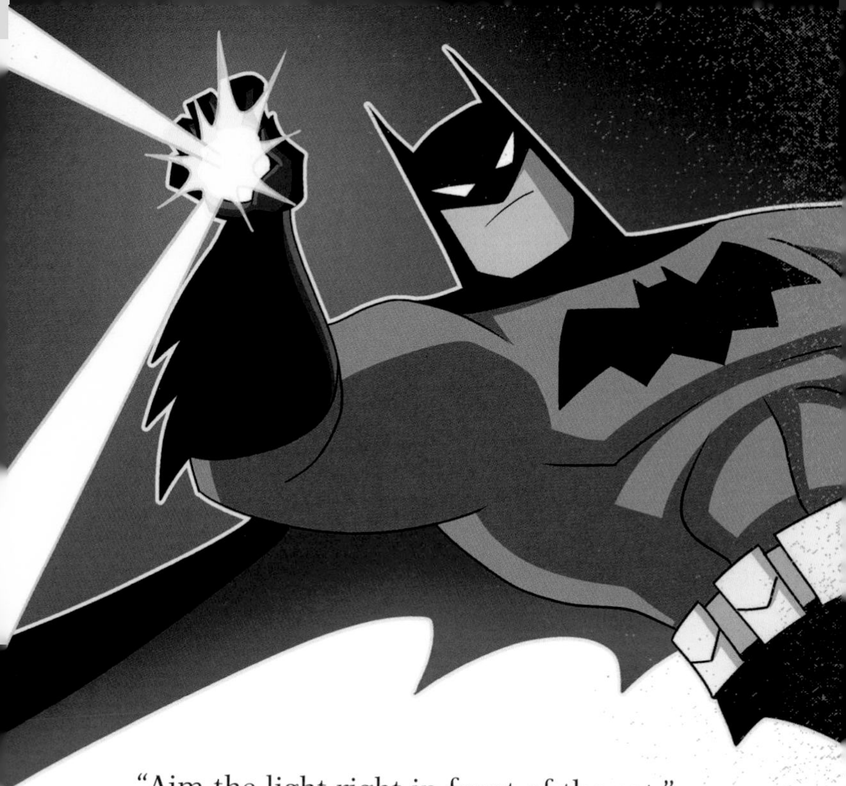

"Aim the light right in front of the cat," says Batman.

The jaguar tilts its head and stares at the two dots of light. The dots bounce across the floor.

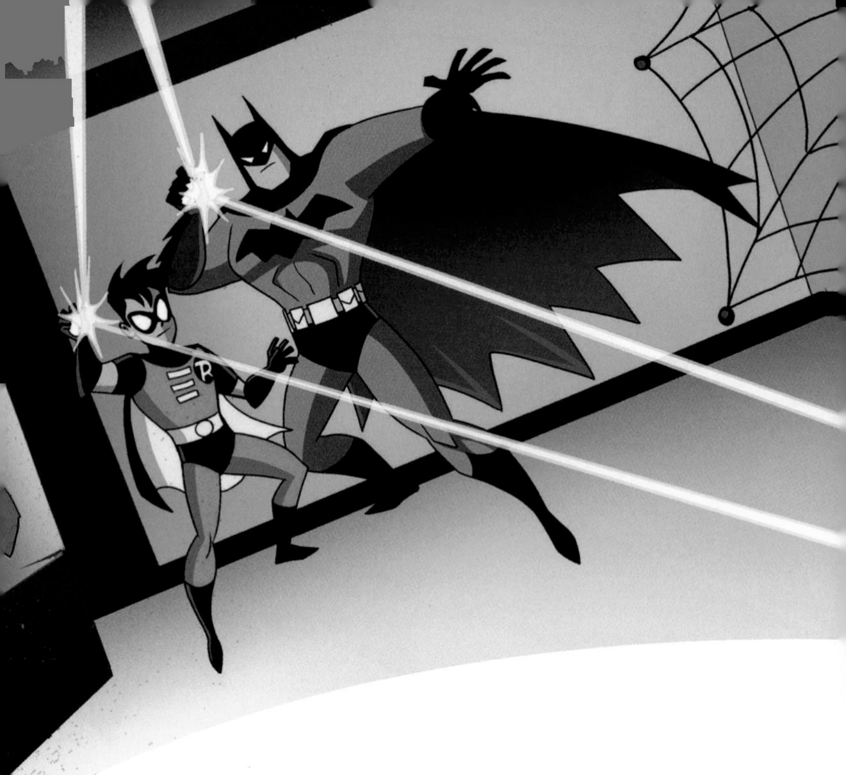

The jaguar pounces at the moving lights.

The Dark Knight quickly removes a device from his Utility Belt. He tosses it toward the cat.

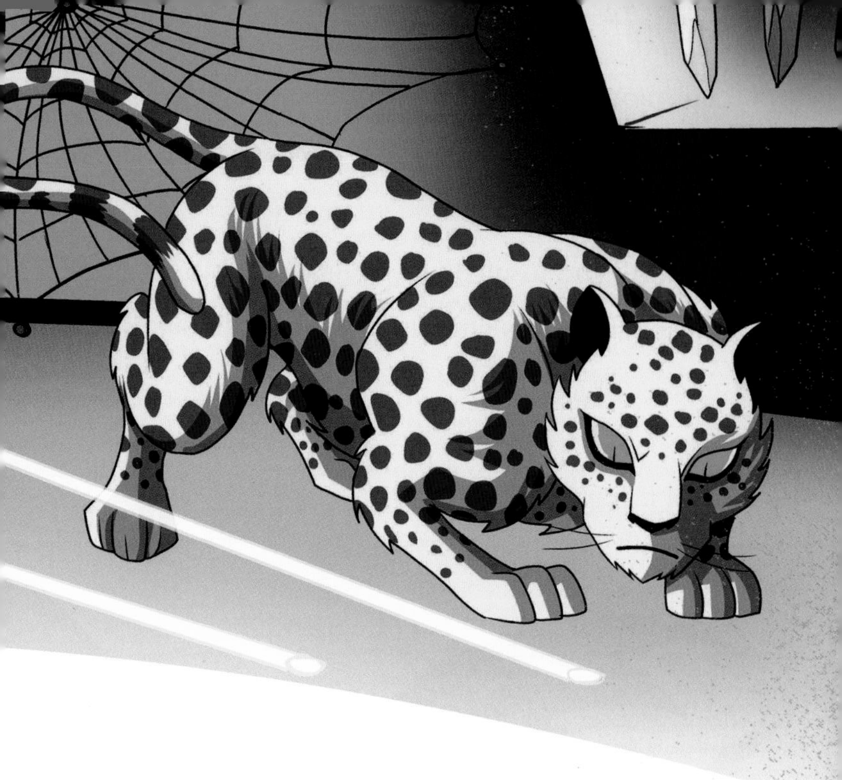

SPPPROINGGG!

A net explodes over the jaguar. It traps the cat within its steely mesh.

Batman grins. “Now to find its owner!”

“I think she went this way,” says Robin. “I heard her heels clicking down this hallway.”

The heroes race out of the room.

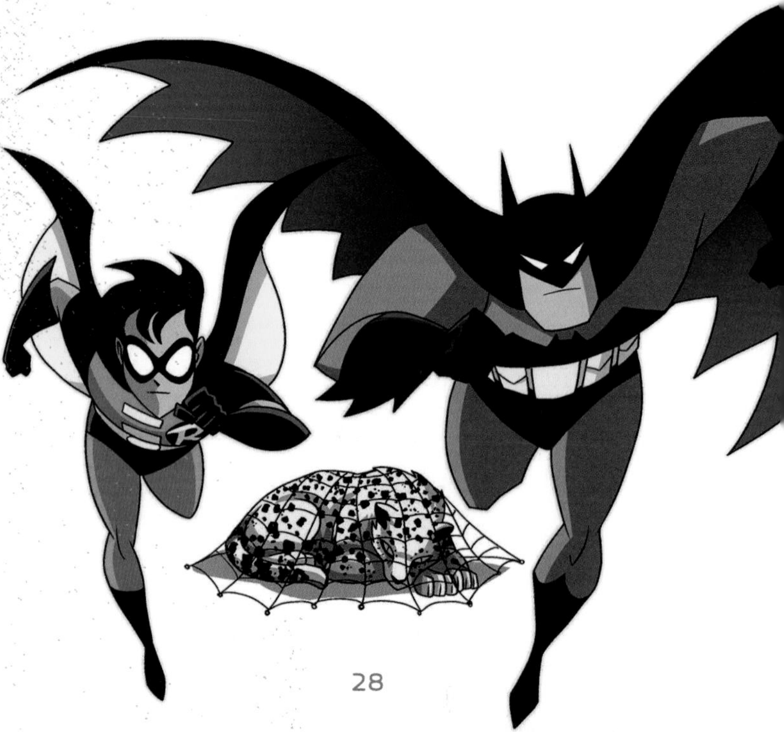

CHAPTER 5

CAT TRICKS

Batman stops in the middle of the hallway.

The listening devices in his cowl pick up a soft sound. It is as soft as a cat's purr.

"She did it again!" exclaims the hero. "Her clicking heels were just another fake-out!"

The Dark Knight pulls a flashlight out of his Utility Belt. He shines it at the ceiling.

Crouching on a ledge near the ceiling is a familiar shape.

"Catwoman!" exclaims Robin.

The villain suddenly leaps over both of the heroes' heads.

But Batman is ready for an escape attempt. He hurls his Batarang at Catwoman. It spins around her with its long, unbreakable rope.

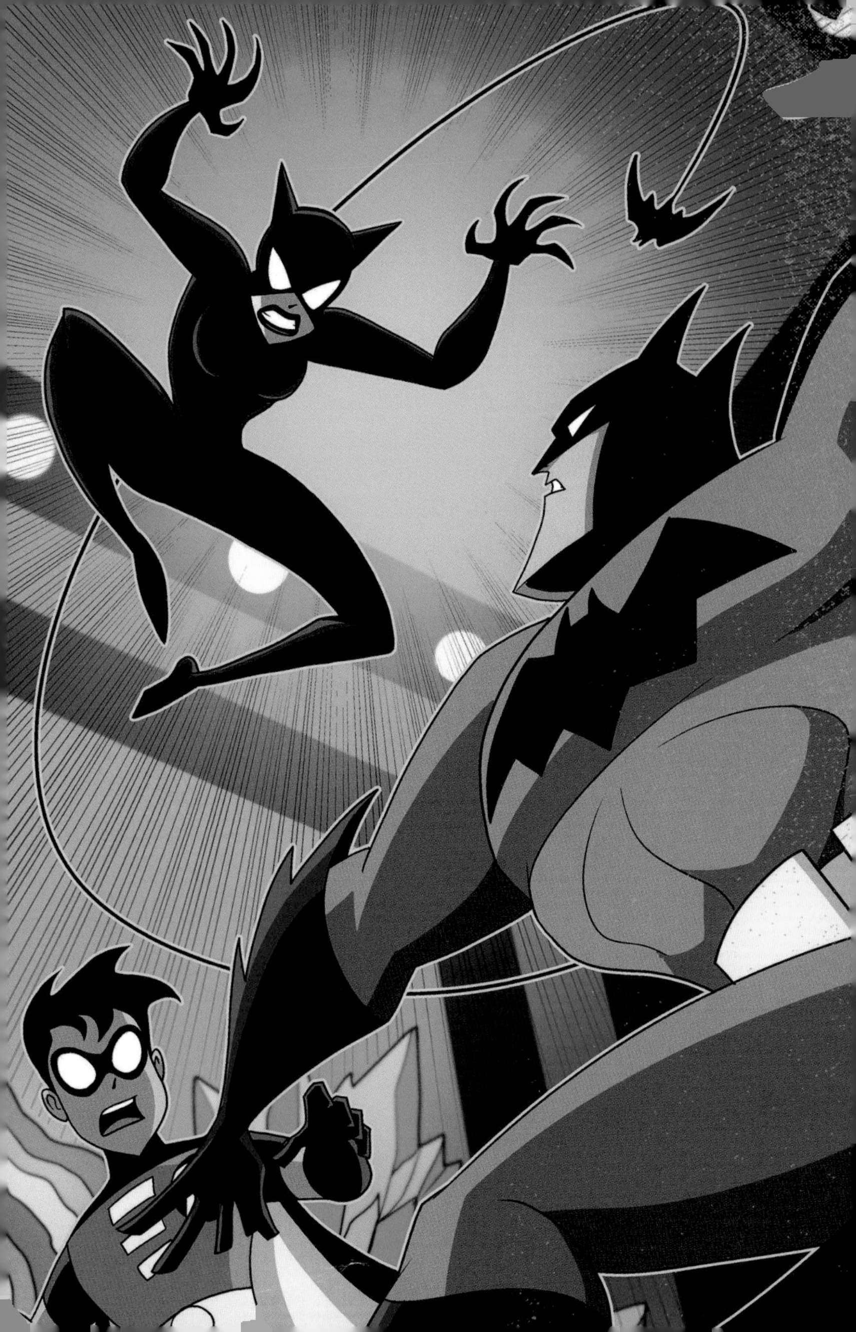

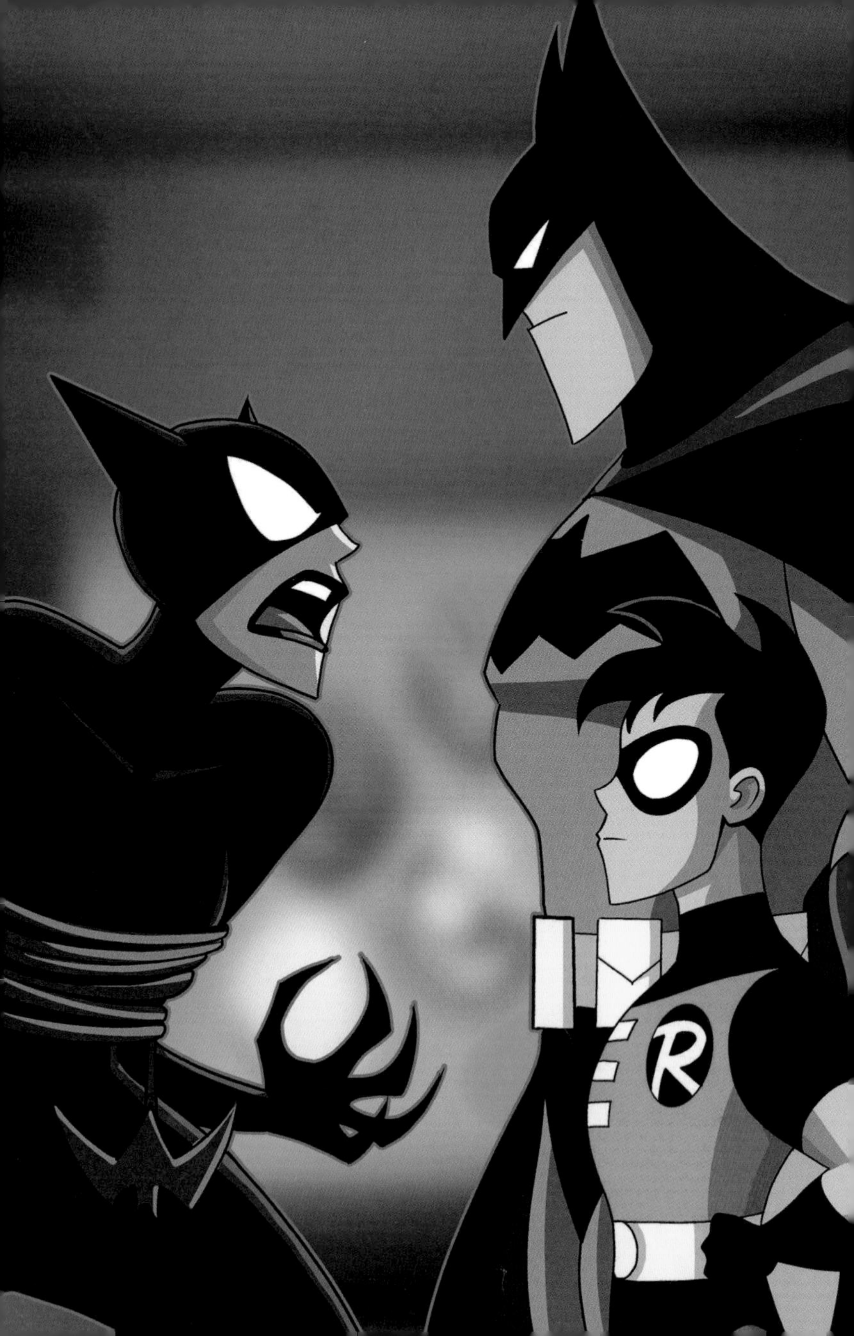

ZINGGGGG!

The thief is trapped just like her jaguar.

ROOOAAAR!

The jaguar's roar echoes through the whole museum.

"Don't you hurt my pet!" says Catwoman.

"Your pet?" Batman says. "It's against the law to bring jaguars into this country. Especially from Bolivia."

"You're going to jail for theft and for smuggling," says Robin.

"Wait!" says Catwoman. She tosses Robin the Jaguar's Jewel.

"I was really on my way back to return the gem," she says.

"Nice try, Catwoman," says Robin. "But your change of heart is as phony as this jewel."

"This jewel is a copy. We planted it the night of the first alarm," says Batman.

"All my hard work for a fake?!" Catwoman hisses angrily.

"The real jewel is locked in the museum safe," Robin says.

"And you'll be locked away safe too . . ." Batman says, ". . . for a real long time!"

EPILOGUE

"Our 3-D printer made the perfect copy of the Jaguar's Jewel. But what should we do with it now, Robin?"

"Let's keep it in the Batcave so we can use it again, Batman."

"Again, Boy Wonder?"

"Yeah, in case there's another jewel thief around — you know, a *copycat*!"

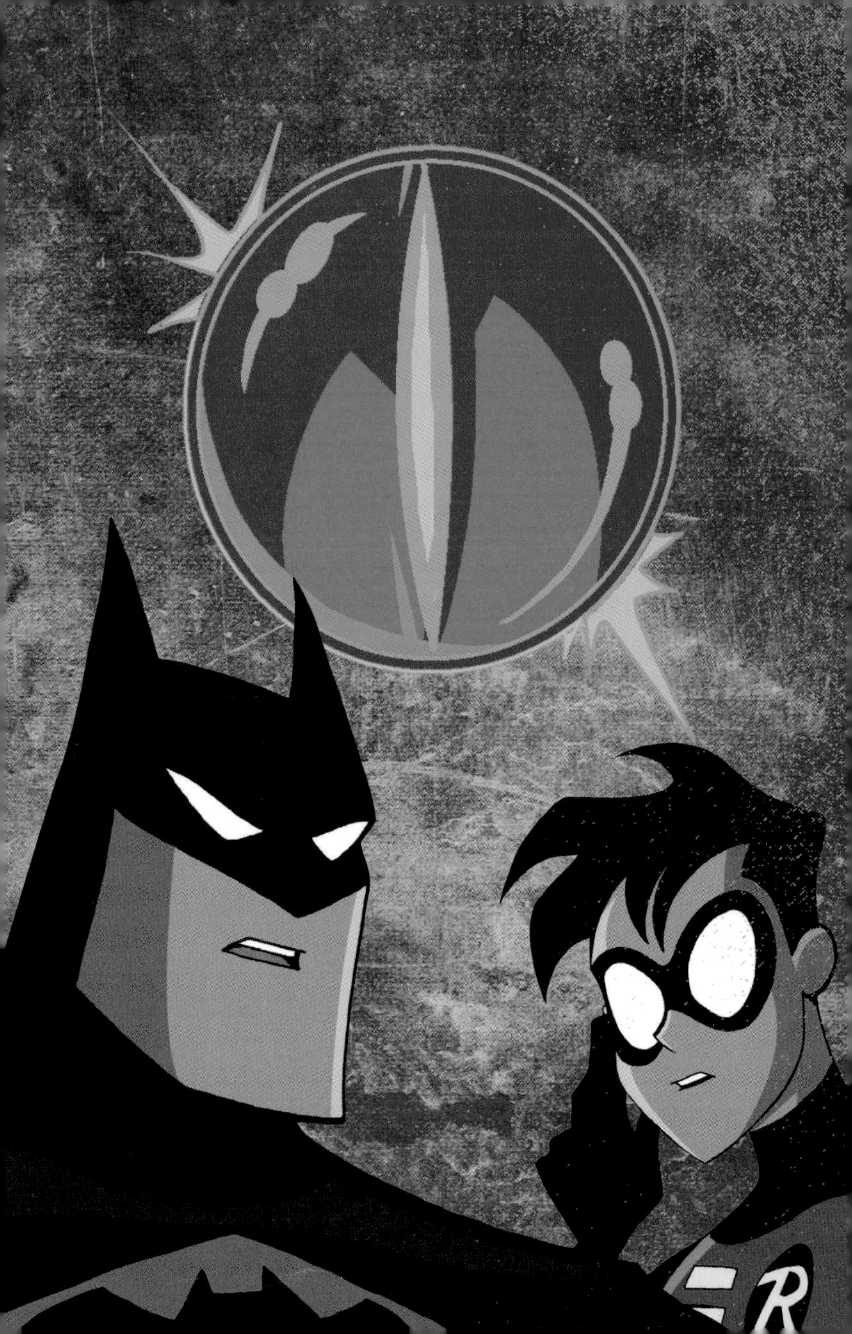

GLOSSARY

catnip (KAT-nip)—a mint plant with a strong scent that cats are attracted to

cowl (KOUL)—a hood or long hooded cloak

device (di-VISSE)—a piece of equipment that does a particular job

disguise (dis-GYZ)—a costume that helps someone hide what they really look like

emerald (EM-ur-uld)—a beautiful gem that is green in color

geology (jee-AHL-uh-jee)—the study of minerals, rocks, and soil

ignore (ig-NOR)—to take no notice of something

jaguar (JAG-wahr)—a large wildcat that is similar to a leopard

mesh (MESH)—a net made of threads or wires

phony (FOHN-ee)—a fake

smuggle (SMUHG-uhl)—to bring something or someone into or out of a country illegally

Discuss

1. What color was the Jaguar's Jewel? Why do you think that was a good color for this special jewel?

2. Batman and Robin hid in the shadows waiting for Catwoman. They were very patient. Have you ever waited for something a long time? What was it? Was it hard to be so patient?

3. In this story the Dynamic Duo and Catwoman keep playing tricks on each other. What were all the different tricks? Discuss which one was your favorite.

Write

1. Catwoman uses a clever disguise to get into the museum and steal the jewel. Can you think of another way she could have tricked her way in? Describe your idea in a few sentences.

2. Batman and Robin use a lot of special tools in their battle against Catwoman. Make a list of them all. Then pick one and write a short description about how you think it works.

3. A real jaguar is Catwoman's pet. What unusual pet would you like to own? Write a paragraph describing it. Include what you would name it and how you would care for it.

Michael Dahl is the prolific author of the
best-selling *Goodnight Baseball* picture book
and more than 200 other books for children
and young adults. He has won the AEP
Distinguished Achievement Award three times
for his nonfiction, a Teachers' Choice Award from
Learning magazine, and a Seal of Excellence from
the Creative Child Awards. He is also the author
of the Hocus Pocus Hotel mystery series and
the Dragonblood books. Dahl currently lives in
Minneapolis, Minnesota.

ILLUSTRATOR

Luciano Vecchio was born in 1982 and is based
in Buenos Aires, Argentina. A freelance artist
for many projects at Marvel and DC Comics, his
work has been seen in print and online around
the world. He has illustrated many DC Super
Heroes books for Capstone, and some of his
recent comic work includes *Beware the Batman*,
Green Lantern: The Animated Series, *Young
Justice*, *Ultimate Spider-Man*, and his creator
owned web-comic, *Sereno*.